CW00864570

Milkman Mike
AND THE RUNAWAY BOTTLES

GREAT NORTHERN

Great Northern Books
PO Box 1380, Bradford, West Yorkshire, BD5 5FB

www.greatnorthernbooks.co.uk

ISBN: 978-1-914227-40-0

Illustrated by Nicky Mills

CIP Data
A catalogue for this book is available from the British Library.

One day Milkman Mike was delivering his milk when suddenly
he saw one of his milk bottles jump up, bounce down from his
pickup called Gold Top 2 and wobble away down the lane!

"Hey!" said Milkman Mike.
"Come back!"

But the milk bottle didn't answer. It just kept on wobbling down the lane towards Farmer Cream's cows.

"And you can stop sniggering!" said Mike, as Spike the big daft dog leaned out of Gold Top 2, laughing.

"Arr, arr, arr? Who? Me?" said Spike.

"Yes, you!" said Mike. "Make yourself useful for a change."

"Arr, arr, arr!" said Spike, saluting, and he dived out of Gold Top 2 and charged after the wobbling bottle.

Milkman Mike stood watching as Spike hurtled down the road. Farmer Cream's cows watched too.

But what was following Spike?
"Oh no!" said Mike.
"There goes another one!"
Another wobbling bottle was now chasing after Spike!

"Spike!" shouted Mike.

Spike turned around to see another wobbling bottle following him!

Spike was confused. Which one should he chase?

"Oh no, again!" said Mike.

Another wobbling bottle
bounced off down the road.

"Spike!" shouted Mike.

"Arr, arr, arr ... Arrr?" said Spike, as five more bottles wobbled by.

What was he to do? He was confused.

"Chase them all!"
said Mike.
"Go on, Spike!"

Nothing else could
go wrong, could it?

Then Spike came back. He ran past Mike.

"Arr, arr, arr," said Spike. "Don't worry!"

"Why?" said Mike.

"Because I am going to get them in Gold Top 2," said Spike.

VROO-OO-OOM! And Gold Top 2 sped by with Spike driving!

It went around the corner.
CRASH!
BANG!
WALLOP!

And all Mike could see was milk, broken bottles and …

"Oh, what's that?" thought Mike.

Mike woke up in his chair, with his big daft dog licking him all over.

"Oh good. I am pleased it was only a dream," said Mike.

"Arr, arr, arr - a dream?" said Spike, as a milk bottle wobbled past them both.

Milkman Mike and Spike are very special to me. I came up with them when telling bedtime stories with my then very young boys, Russell and Stewart.

These books are dedicated to my wonderful wife Pauline, our now grown-up children Russell, Stewart & Caroline, their partners Alexandra, Sophie & Tom – and our two grandchildren Amelia (Mimi) and Isabella.

Finally, a massive thank you to Nicky Mills who has brought Milkman Mike and Spike to life through her excellent illustrations – and to my publishers Great Northern Books and particularly David Burrill for his support.

We look forward to bringing you more adventures in the future!

Chris

Also available in the Milkman Mike series

Milkman Mike and the Spaceship

Milkman Mike and the Fire Engine

Milkman Mike and the Football Match

www.greatnorthernbooks.co.uk